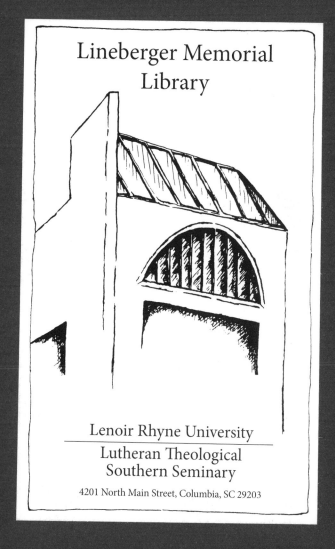

Lineberger Memorial
Library

Lenoir Rhyne University

Lutheran Theological
Southern Seminary

4201 North Main Street, Columbia, SC 29203

Who Counts?

100 Sheep, 10 Coins, and 2 Sons

Amy-Jill Levine & Sandy Eisenberg Sasso
Illustrated by Margaux Meganck

With a Note to Parents and Teachers

WJK WESTMINSTER
JOHN KNOX PRESS
LOUISVILLE • KENTUCKY

One Hundred Sheep

One hundred sheep! If just a single one were lost, who would notice? Who counted sheep anyway? The man did. The man had a lot of sheep, one hundred of them. He counted them every day.

He kept counting:

It took time to count, a long time.

One day the man counted: 10 20 30 40

91

92 93 94

Then he stopped.

There were only ninety-nine! He must have made a mistake; he had one hundred sheep, not ninety-nine. He counted again.

Still there were only ninety-nine.

One of his sheep was missing! He was responsible for ALL the sheep, all one hundred of them.

Immediately the man went to look for the lost sheep. He walked and walked, but he saw nothing. He kept walking. He looked to the left. Nothing.

He looked to the right. Nothing. He walked and he listened.

Still nothing. Then he heard it: a bleating sound.

BAA!

He ran toward the sound. And there she was—the lost sheep!

He had found her.

She was too tired to follow him home,

so he lifted her on his shoulders and carried her.

He was so happy to have all his sheep together that he invited everyone to celebrate.

Some people said, "What's so wonderful? It was only one sheep. You had ninety-nine others." The man smiled. "One sheep makes a difference. Without her, something is missing. Now my flock is complete."

Ten Coins

Ten drachmas, ten silver coins.

Every day the woman would count them.

Then one day she counted.

She stopped. She couldn't have made a mistake, but she counted again anyway. Still she counted only nine. One drachma was missing. She had lost one of her coins.

The woman lit a lamp to see more clearly. She looked under chairs and in corners. No coin!

She looked in cabinets and in wastebaskets. Still no drachma! She took a broom and swept the floor. There were crumbs and dust, but no coin! It was her fault.

She had lost the coin, and now she must find it. She searched
again with the light and the broom.

Finally, she saw something shining and heard a ping. She looked down, and there it was—the missing coin!

She held the coin in her hand for a few moments,
and then she carefully placed it with the other drachmas.

She was so happy to have all the coins that she invited the women in the town to celebrate. Some people said, "What is so important? It was only one coin." The woman smiled. "Just one coin matters. Without it, something is missing. Now my coin collection is complete."

Two Sons

A father had two sons.

Easier to count than ten, much easier than one hundred.

One day the younger son wanted half his father's money. It would be his eventually, but he could not wait. He was restless, and he wanted to travel. So the father divided his wealth in half and gave half to his younger son and half to his older son.

The younger son went to a foreign land.
There he had a great time doing whatever he wanted.

But before long he had spent all the money and had none left, not even to pay for food. There was no one to share even a crumb of bread with him, as there was little food in the land.

The son went to work for a farmer to try to earn enough to buy something to eat. The farmer told him to go and feed the pigs.

Even the pods that the pigs ate looked good.

Finally, the son was so hungry and tired that he decided to return to his father. But he wasn't sure what to say. How could he tell his father that he had spent all the money?

His good pants were torn. His shirt was stained. His fancy shoes had holes. He thought, "I will tell my father that I made a big mistake. I will say that I am sorry. I will offer to work hard to earn money."

The young son returned home. His hair was uncombed, his face was dirty, and his hands were covered in blisters.

His father ran to greet him. He was so happy to see him that he did not care about anything else.

Instead of making his son earn money for clothing and food, he gave him a new coat, new shoes, and even a new ring.

Then he invited everyone to *his* home to celebrate.

The older son was still working in the field when he heard the happy sounds of singing and laughter and smelled sweet spices coming from his home. He wondered what was happening.

He stopped one of the neighbors who was heading to his house and asked, "What is going on?"

The neighbor was surprised by the question. "Don't you know that your father is making a big party for your brother to mark his return?" The older brother did not know.

When the father counted everyone who had come to the party, he realized that one person was missing.

That person was his older son! He had forgotten to invite him.

He ran out of his house
to find his son.

When the older son
saw his father coming
toward him, he turned
away. He was sad and
angry that no one had
come to find him.

His father spoke softly. "Your brother has come home. I invited all our friends to celebrate with us. You must come and be glad with us." He tried to hug his son, but his son folded his arms across his chest.

The older son finally said to his father, "I have been with you all the years that my brother has been away. I did not waste your money. I did everything you wanted me to do. I never left you, but my brother did. Then you make a big party for him. You never had one for me. You didn't even invite me to his."

The father thought, "I have two sons—one, two. I paid attention to my younger son, but I discounted my older son. I didn't realize that he felt lost."

The father took his older son's hands in his own. "Please come and join the party. I love you. All I have is yours. Come and be with me and with your brother."

"I have TWO sons."

He counted—"one"—and he pointed to the house where his younger son was celebrating. He counted—"two"—and he put his arms around his older son.

"Without you," he said, "something is missing. With you, our family is complete."

A Note to Parents and Teachers

A parable is a simple story that asks us to think about very important matters: our relationships with others, our place in the world, how we can be better people.

Who Counts? retells three parables from the New Testament's Gospel of Luke, chapter 15.

In the Christian tradition, these stories are called the Parable of the Lost Sheep or the Parable of the Good Shepherd, the Parable of the Lost Coin, and the Parable of the Prodigal Son. The Gospel did not give these titles to the stories. Later interpreters called them by those names.

When the church was separating itself from Judaism, some Christian interpreters erroneously explained these stories as indicating the difference between the "stern" and "angry" God of the Jews and the "forgiving" and "merciful" God of the Christians. That is not what the original stories were designed to do. God in both traditions is merciful and forgiving. Jesus was a Jewish teacher, and he, along with his fellow Jews, viewed God as loving.

The Christian tradition has sometimes understood the parables to be allegories. It made connections between details in the parables and people or events in the world. For example, the sheep, the coin, and the prodigal son represent repenting sinners; the man who seeks the lost sheep and the father who welcomes the prodigal son are symbols for God. Ironically, the tradition less often sees the woman who seeks her coin as a symbol for God.

Our presentation of these parables does not intend to erase the focus on repenting and forgiving. Rather, we seek to add a new understanding based on what we imagine Jesus' original audiences would have heard. That audience would not think that the man who lost his sheep, the woman who lost her coin, or the father who lost his older son were symbols for God. This is because God doesn't lose us. Nor would they think of the sheep and the coin as examples of repenting, because sheep and coins don't repent.

In our reading, the three stories are connected. The first two stories set up the third. The main message is about counting, searching for what is missing, and celebrating becoming whole again.

The shepherd counts the sheep; that is the only way he would know one is missing. The woman counts the coins so that she is aware when one has been lost. Finally, the father realizes that although his younger son has returned, he has lost his older son. The sheep is returned, and the coin is found. Whether the older son will recognize his father's love remains an open question.

When we read parables, we should ask ourselves: Where am I in this story? How am I like the man who lost his sheep, the woman who lost her coin, the father who feels he may have lost both his sons? Do I ever feel like the lost one? How am I like the younger brother who does not want to stay home? How am I like the older brother who does everything his father tells him but who does not feel that he is loved?

The parable then prompts other questions: Have I lost something, or someone, and not paid attention? Is there someone I take for granted? What, or whom, have I forgotten to count?

If we take these questions seriously and act on them, we are better able to love our neighbors as ourselves (Lev. 19:18, quoted in Matt. 19:19; 22:39; Mark 12:31; Gal. 5:14).

Amy-Jill Levine is University Professor of New Testament and Jewish Studies, E. Rhodes and Leona B. Carpenter Professor of New Testament Studies, and Professor of Jewish Studies at Vanderbilt Divinity School and College of Arts and Science. For more details on the parables, see her *Short Stories by Jesus: The Enigmatic Parables of a Controversial Rabbi* (HarperOne, 2014).

Sandy Eisenberg Sasso is the Director of Religion, Spirituality and the Arts Initiative at Butler University and Christian Theological Seminary, Rabbi Emerita of Congregation Beth-El Zedeck, and an author of many award-winning children's books.

Margaux Meganck is a freelance artist and children's book illustrator in Portland, Oregon. She is a member of the Society of Children's Book Writers and Illustrators.

© 2017 Amy-Jill Levine and Sandy Eisenberg Sasso
Illustrations © 2017 Margaux Meganck

First edition
Published by Westminster John Knox Press
Louisville, Kentucky

17 18 19 20 21 22 23 24 25 26—10 9 8 7 6 5 4 3 2 1

Book design by Allison Taylor | Cover design by Allison Taylor
Cover illustration by Margaux Meganck

Library of Congress Cataloging-in-Publication Data
Names: Levine, Amy-Jill, 1956- author. | Sasso, Sandy Eisenberg, author.
Title: Who counts? : 100 sheep, 10 coins, and 2 sons / Amy-Jill Levine
  and Sandy Eisenberg Sasso.
Description: Louisville, KY : Westminster John Knox Press, 2017.
Identifiers: LCCN 2016052021 | ISBN 9780664262747 (pbk. : alk. paper)
Subjects: LCSH: Jesus Christ--Parables--Juvenile literature. |
  Self-esteem--Religious aspects--Christianity--Juvenile literature.
Classification: LCC BT376 .L48 2017 | DDC 226.8/06--dc23 LC record available
  at https://lccn.loc.gov/2016052021

PRINTED IN CHINA